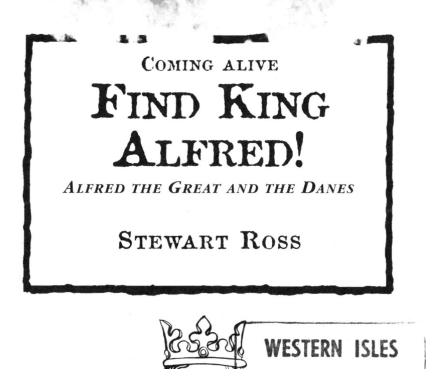

COMING ALIVE

FIND KING ALFRED!

ALFRED THE GREAT AND THE DANES

STEWART ROSS

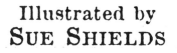

Illustrated by
SUE SHIELDS

Evans

NS BROTHI

TO THE READER

Find King Alfred! is a story. It is based on history. The main events in the book really happened. But some of the details, such as what people said, are made up. I hope this makes the story more fun to read. I also hope that *Find King Alfred!* will get you interested in real history. When you have finished, perhaps you will want to find out more about Alfred the Great and the Danes.

Stewart Ross

For Alex, with love.

Published by Evans Brothers Limited
2A Portman Mansions, Chiltern Street
London W1M 1LE

© copyright in the text Stewart Ross 1998
© copyright in the illustrations Sue Shields 1998

British Library Cataloguing in Publication Data
Ross, Stewart
Find King Alfred! – (Coming alive)
1. Alfred, King of England – Juvenile literature
2. Great Britain – History – Alfred 871-899 – Juvenile literature
I. Title
942'.0164'092

First published 1998

Printed in Spain by Gráficas Reunidas, S.A.

0 237 51786 8

CONTENTS

THE STORY SO FAR...

ANGLO-SAXON ENGLAND

After the Romans left England, tribes of Angles and Saxons arrived from Europe. They settled down in small kingdoms. The most important were Northumbria, Mercia and Wessex (the West Saxons).

In 597 Christianity came to England. The Anglo-Saxons built churches and set up schools. Towns and markets grew. The kings ruled well and over the years England became richer and more peaceful.

THE VIKINGS

Disaster came to Anglo-Saxon England in 793. Viking warriors from Scandinavia (Denmark, Norway and Sweden) began to raid the country. They were a tough, violent people, who worshipped strange gods such as Odin and Thor. Their cruel ways struck terror into Anglo-Saxon hearts.

The first Vikings came to England for plunder. Later groups settled down. One by one, the Anglo-Saxon kingdoms fell to the Vikings. By 875 only Wessex was left.

Alfred, son of King Ethelwulf, was born in 849. He travelled in Europe when he was young. As a grown-up he spent most of his time fighting Vikings from Denmark (the Danes). In 871, when his brother Ethelred died, Alfred became king of Wessex.

For seven years Alfred held on to Wessex. Sometimes the Saxons beat the Danes in battle, sometimes they paid them to go away. But by the winter of 877-8, things were looking grim. A huge Danish army was camped at Gloucester. One of its leaders, King Guthrum, was looking greedily towards Wessex ...

King Alfred   **King Guthrum**

Portrait gallery

King Guthrum

King Alfred

Ivan

Ubbe the Fool

The Saxon priest

The Saxon merchant

Earl Athelnorth

Plegmund

CHAPTER ONE

GUTHRUM'S FEAST

'Silence!' Guthrum the Dane hammered his huge fist on the table.

'Warriors of the North, stand and drink a toast with me!' he roared. He raised his jewelled drinking cup high in the air. 'Death to King Alfred! Death to Alfred and all other puny Saxons!'

King Guthrum

Guthrum's warriors rose to their feet. 'Death to Alfred!' they yelled. Time and again the shouts echoed around the roof of the great hall. Guthrum looked down the tables. What a great band they are! he thought. By this time next year I'll rule all Wessex. By Odin's burning eye I will!

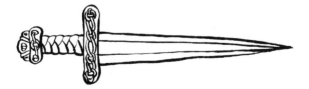

The king sat down and grabbed a hunk of venison. 'Excuse me, O Orphan-maker,' said a voice at his side. 'May a humble worm have a word with you?'

Guthrum looked round. It was the club-footed warrior known as Ubbe the Fool. Although useless in battle, he was said to be the wisest man in the army. But he had an annoying habit of making his advice sound like nonsense.

Ubbe the Fool

'You know the Saxons are nettles, O King of the Axe-swingers?'

'Eh?' Guthrum grunted.

'The more you cut them down, the more they grow!'

Guthrum wiped his mouth on his sleeve. 'Not when I've finished with them, they don't!'

Ubbe smiled. Stepping back, he began to sing: 'A Viking is fighting all day long. But he can't beat Saxons, says my song!'

'Shut up! You blithering wind-bag!' shouted Guthrum.

Ubbe looked sideways at the king. 'Temper, temper! Let me finish. You'll be sorry if you don't.' He went on: 'You might bury Alfred in the sod, but one man you can't kill is his god!'

A look of fury crossed Guthrum's face. He stood up and grasped Ubbe round the throat. 'What in the name of Odin do you mean?' he hissed.

'What in the name of Odin do you mean?'
he hissed.

'Hurrrgh!' gurgled the Fool. 'How can I talk with your hairy great hand on my windpipe? Let go and I'll tell you.'

Guthrum removed his hand. Ubbe sat at the table and waited for the king to join him. 'All I want to suggest, O Wonder-warrior,' he began, 'is this ...'

Ubbe the Fool   **King Guthrum**

The two men talked for half an hour. When they had finished, Guthrum rose and once again hammered on the table for silence. He looked pale and determined. 'Men', he began, 'listen carefully. The feast is over. Turn in now and get some sleep. You'll need the rest, for tomorrow we move against Wessex!'

At first the Danes did not believe what they had heard. 'Attack Wessex in the middle of *winter?*' cried Ivan, a huge man with a scar that ran from his neck to his left eye. 'You can't be serious, Guffrum!'

Ivan

'Yes, Ivan, I'm deadly serious. Surprise is the secret of war. Alfred and his men won't be expecting us until the spring. We'll catch them napping, slay them like lambs and feed their flesh to the crows! Then we'll know who's stronger' - he cast a furious glance at Ubbe - 'the mighty Odin or the Saxons' wimpy Jesus Christ!'

The feast broke up immediately and servants cleared the tables. Wrapping their cloaks about them, the warriors lay down on the floor to sleep. As Guthrum was making himself comfortable, he looked over to where Ubbe lay. 'Well, Fool,' he growled, 'what do you think?'

'It is not what I suggested.'

'You gave girls' advice. Make peace, indeed!'

'Hey-ho,' sighed Ubbe. 'Kings always know best.'

'That's why they are kings,' said Guthrum grumpily.

'Of course. I forgot that. How stupid of me! But I think you will make three mistakes, O Saxonslayer. Goodnight.'

Guthrum did not reply. But as he closed his eyes, he heard Ubbe singing softly in the darkness, 'You might bury Alfred in the sod ...'

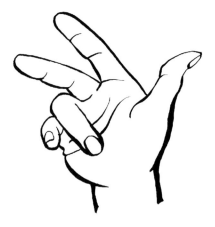

CHAPTER TWO

'WHERE IS YOUR KING?'

The Danes left Gloucester shortly after dawn. They rode into the dull red sun towards the Saxon town of Chippenham. From prisoners they learned that King Alfred had spent Christmas there. Guthrum reckoned if they moved fast they could take the king of Wessex before he had time to escape.

They reached the Cotswolds at midday. On the grassy slopes they came across a shepherd and his family huddled together in a small hut. Before Guthrum could stop him, Ivan had killed them all and set fire to their home.

Ubbe watched the black smoke rise into the still, frosty air. 'Mistake number one, O son of Odin,' he muttered. Guthrum glared at him. Ubbe went on, 'I wonder if the smoke can be seen in Chippenham?'

Mistake number one

'Be quiet, Fool,' the king replied crossly. Without another word, he ordered his men to ride on.

As the light was fading, the Danes crossed the overgrown Fosse Way. When they were gone, a man rose from the bushes by the roadside and galloped off to the south. Five minutes later he turned to the left along the frozen track that led to Chippenham.

The Danes halted for the night on the banks of the River Avon. Guthrum ordered no fires to be lit - he was still hoping to surprise Alfred. The army rose before dawn. As they sharpened their swords, they boasted about the deeds they would do that day. Ivan bet half an ox he would kill all the priests in the town. 'And to prove it I'll skewer their heads on spears for everyone to see!' he laughed.

Ivan

During the night the weather had changed. It was now chilly and damp, and a thick mist hung over the ground. Leaving their horses, the Danes advanced the last half-mile on foot.

Most of the people of Chippenham were still in bed when the Danes burst in. Many died where they lay. A small band of Saxon soldiers battled

Most of the people of Chippenham
were still in bed when the Danes burst in.
Many died where they lay.

on in front of the church before they were hacked to pieces and their bodies thrown into the river. By mid-morning, when the sun finally broke through, Guthrum's victory was complete.

The few dozen Saxons who were left alive - mostly terrified women and children - were herded together at the end of the main street. With Ivan and Ubbe on either side of him, Guthrum stood on an upturned barrel and spoke to them. 'Saxon scum,' he snarled, 'where is your king?'

No one spoke.

'Right. Bring me that wrinkled wreck!' Guthrum pointed to an elderly prisoner at the back of the crowd. Two Danes stepped forward and dragged the man before the king.

'Now, old fool, answer me!'

The Saxon priest

Ubbe the Fool

Looking him straight in the eye, the Saxon said something in a strange language. Guthrum looked blank. He turned to Ubbe. 'Is the old fool mad?'

'No, O son of Odin. He's speaking Latin.'

'Huh! What did he say?'

Ubbe looked awkward. 'He said, "Father forgive them. They do not know what they are doing." '

King Guthrum

'Don't know what I'm doing!' exploded Guthrum. 'By Odin's bloody sword! Kill him!'

When the deed was done, Guthrum calmed down. He asked Ubbe why the man had spoken Latin. 'That's his language,' Ubbe replied. 'All Christian priests speak Latin.'

'You mean he was a priest?' interrupted Ivan, who was standing nearby.

'Yes.'

Ivan swore. 'Bother you, Guffrum! You've made me lose my bet!'

CHAPTER THREE

'MERCY!'

Guthrum soon realised that Alfred had escaped. Warned that the Danes were coming, the king of Wessex had left Chippenham during the night. Guthrum was annoyed. Even so, he was sure he would have his enemy at his mercy before long.

King Guthrum

The Danes' first task was to make themselves safe by building a fort. Guthrum chose a strong position on a bend of the River Avon. It was protected on three sides by water. On the fourth side his men put up a huge wall of earth and

wood. The king was delighted with the work. Not even the hall of the gods, he said, was as well protected as the Danish army in Wessex.

Now they had a secure base, the Danes began raiding the countryside all around. It was Ivan's favourite work. Leading a band of warriors, he rode fast to a town or monastery, attacked it and returned with his plunder before the Saxons knew what  had hit them. They killed all the poor people they met. Priests, merchants and noblemen were taken prisoner. They were more valuable alive than dead. Guthrum did not mind them buying their freedom - as long as they paid handsomely and accepted him as their king.

King Alfred

Within a few weeks a large part of Wessex was under his control. Some Saxons fled abroad. Others came to the Danish king and made peace with him. But of Alfred there was still no sign.

One evening in early March Ivan rode into the fort towing a chubby merchant behind him. The man was clearly not used to exercise. When Ivan halted, the prisoner collapsed to the ground in a sweating heap. Guthrum strode up and kicked him.

The Saxon merchant

'Mercy!' the fellow blubbered. 'O great Dane, have mercy!'

'I don't speak very good Saxon, whale flesh,' Guthrum laughed. 'Tell me, what does "mercy" mean?'

The man peered up at him with piggy eyes. 'The holy gospel says "Blessed are the merciful", sir.'

'Gospel? Blessed? What in the name of Odin are you jabbering about?' asked Guthrum. He gave the man another kick.

Ubbe stepped forward and explained, 'The gospel is the Christians' holy book, Great King. It

King Guthrum

Ubbe the Fool

King Guthrum

says that kind people are blessed, which means they go to heaven. Odd, isn't it?'

'Odd?' shouted Guthrum. 'It's downright stupid! Heaven is for warriors, not weeds. If I were soft and kind, *I* would be lying on the ground instead of this greasy lard-bag.' To prove his point, he stood on the merchant's fingers.

'Ow! Please let me go and I will do anything,' he whimpered.

'That's what they all say,' Guthrum sneered, 'until they hear what I want.'

The merchant lifted his head. 'What *do* you want, dear Dane?'

'Where is your king?'

The merchant hesitated. 'I - I don't know.'

'Just as I thought,' replied Guthrum. 'They're all the same.' He turned to a group of warriors. 'Take this toad away. Lean on him a bit to see if he's telling the truth. Then, if he's still alive, he can pay fifty gold pieces and go free.'

Before the men could move, the merchant grabbed Guthrum's ankles. 'No more pain!' he screamed. 'I'll tell you everything. Alfred is hiding in the marshes. Near Athelney. With Earl Athelnorth.'

If I were soft and kind, *I* would be lying on the ground instead of this greasy lard-bag.'

A broad grin spread across Guthrum's face. 'Thank you, toad. Thank you very much. I'll be merciful now, then we'll both go to heaven, won't we?'

CHAPTER FOUR

'FIND KING ALFRED!'

Ivan and his warband set
out for Athelney the
next day. Before they
left, Guthrum took
their leader to one
side. 'I have only two
things to say to you,
Ivan.'

'Two?' asked the warrior
anxiously. He had never been
very good at maths.

'One. Don't get caught up in any unnecessary
fights.'

Ivan looked upset. 'Oh! Come off it, Guffrum.
Can't we even stop for a bit of pillage?'

'No. And beware of surprise attacks. Don't
underestimate your enemy.'

'Don't what?'

'Don't think Alfred is weak,' Guthrum
explained.

'Ah!' Ivan nodded. 'Sure I won't underesterlate
him, Guffrum. I'll mince him instead. Ha-ha-ha!'

'No!' burst out Guthrum. 'By Odin's blazing
sword, Ivan! Don't you ever think of anything but
fighting?'

'No, sire.' Ivan paused a moment. 'Well, I do sometimes think of drinking.'

'Well try something new for once. You are not going to fight Alfred. Your orders are to find out exactly where he is, how strong his fort is, how many men he has and so on.'

King Alfred

'One: where is he?' repeated Ivan, counting on his fingers. 'Two: how strong is his fort? Three: how many men? Four: and so on ...'

'Forget it,' Guthrum snorted. 'Just remember this: Find King Alfred! That's all.'

'No problem, Guffrum,' grinned Ivan. 'I can almost smell him from here.'

That afternoon Guthrum and Ubbe took a walk along the bank of the Avon. After they had gone a little way, Ubbe asked, 'Why is Alfred like a river?'

'Forget it,' Guthrum snorted.
'Just remember this: Find King Alfred!
That's all.'

Guthrum scratched his head. 'Because he's wet?'

Ubbe laughed. 'Good try, O Wessex-crusher! But the real answer is: Because he's always running away!'

The Danish king groaned. 'Haven't you got anything better to do than make up silly riddles, Fool?' He turned to go back to the fort. Ubbe put a hand on his sleeve.

'It's not such a bad idea, is it, O Merchant-mangler?'

'What isn't?'

'Running away. Take Alfred, for example ...'

'Take Alfred? Yes, I will! And when I have him, I'll make him sorry he was ever born!'

Ubbe looked away and began to hum to himself. 'You might bury Alf...'

Ubbe the Fool

King Guthrum

32

Guthrum turned purple with fury. 'If you sing that ditty again, Fool,' he shouted, 'I'll have you torn apart by horses!'

Ubbe stopped at once and the two men walked back to the fort in silence.

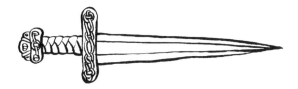

Ivan and his warband returned a week later. As they entered the fort, Guthrum noticed that several men were missing. He soon found out what had happened.

The Danes had followed the Vale of Malmsbury as far as the Mendip Hills. From there they went to Glastonbury, where Ivan promised they would find plunder. They arrived to find the place deserted and everything of value gone. Pushing on across the low, marshy ground, they came to the Polden Hills. Here they got lost.

Wandering about in the lonely woods, they had an eerie feeling they were being watched. Then the murders started. First it was a man who had gone off to find water. They discovered his headless body by a stream. Next half a dozen men were killed as they looked for firewood. So the attacks went on, with never a sign of the enemy.

In the end, even Ivan lost his nerve and decided to go home. As the Danes started out across the marshes, a figure appeared at the edge of the woods behind them. 'Go, heathen!' it shouted. 'And tell this to your leader: Christ and King Alfred will triumph!'

Chapter five

WHISPERINGS

Guthrum was worried by what had happened to Ivan's warband. It was the first time things had gone wrong for him in Wessex. His men had been made fools of, and he still did not know exactly where Alfred was. But he did know that the Saxon leader was clever and well-organised. He probably had a strong army, too.

King Alfred

Over the following days a change came over the Saxons. Merchants stopped begging Guthrum to be their king. When Danish

warbands appeared, farmers no longer fled into the woods. They locked themselves in their houses and fought back. Some of those who had gone abroad returned home. No one seemed afraid of the Danes any more.

Ivan

Christian crosses began to appear in the most unlikely places. They were carved on trees. During the night one was cut in the grass outside the fort. Ivan even found one scratched on to his helmet. He thought it was a love message from a serving girl. He was furious when Ubbe told him what it really was.

There were whisperings, too. Prisoners muttered together in the darkness of the hut where they were held. Slaves spoke secretly in shadowy corners. In the villages that Guthrum ruled, Saxons uttered strange greetings in the street. Not many Danes spoke their language well. But they all knew the word that cropped up in every whispered conversation. Alfred.

King Guthrum

'Alfred! Alfred! Alfred!' grumbled Guthrum one morning. He looked tired. 'I am sick and tired of him and his wretched Christianity, Ubbe. He's

Prisoners muttered together in the darkness
of the hut where they were held.

everywhere and nowhere. How can we fight an enemy we can't get hold of?'

Earl Athelnorth

The previous day Earl Athelnorth had ambushed a Danish warband at Broad Ford to the south. Guthrum's men had easily fought their way out of trouble. But as they retreated, someone had shouted after them: 'Christ and Alfred will triumph!' It was the same cry as Ivan had heard in the marshes.

'It can't be done,' said Ubbe after a while.

'What can't, Fool?'

'You can't fight an enemy you can't get hold of. I don't think even Odin can behead a ghost.' Ubbe began cleaning his fingernails with his knife.

'You know, Fool,' said Guthrum slowly, 'I sometimes feel I've had enough of fighting.'

'Mmm. Me too.' Ubbe put down his knife. 'Would you like me to be a fly, O Widow-maker?'

'What in the name of thunder are you talking about?'

Ubbe stood up. 'Disguise myself as a Saxon.

Buzz around a bit. Find out what's really going on?'

The king jumped at the idea and decided that Ubbe should slip out of the fort that night. As the Fool left to get ready, he called over his shoulder, 'By the way, O Christ-crusher, sending Ivan to find Alfred was mistake number two.' Guthrum groaned.

Mistake number two

Three days later Ubbe was back. He reported to Guthrum immediately. Alfred had left his fort in the marshes and had ordered the men of Wessex to gather at Egbert's Stone, ready for war. The Saxons were going to attack!

'At last!' Guthrum cried. 'A chance to meet this cursed Alfred and slice him to pieces. Then all Wessex will be mine!'

Ubbe the Fool

Ubbe gave him an odd look. 'Excuse me, O Saxon-slaughterer, but I thought you had had enough of fighting?'

'Enough fighting? I can never get enough fighting!' roared Guthrum, snatching up his sword.

'Ah well! I must be going deaf,' muttered Ubbe. 'But I think you are about to make mistake number three.'

CHAPTER SIX

JUST A TINY ARMY!

Ubbe had never seen Guthrum so excited. The fight with Alfred promised to be the most important of his whole life. If he won and Alfred was killed, then Wessex would be Danish and Guthrum would be its king. If he lost ... No one thought of losing. Except Ubbe, and he said nothing.

Guthrum divided his army into three. He left one group in the fort, commanded by Anund and Ubbe. Ivan led the second group. Their job was to spread out ahead of Guthrum and find out where the Saxons were. Guthrum's group followed Ivan's, ready to move forward when the enemy had been found. It was a sensible plan. But it would work only if everyone obeyed orders.

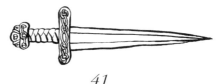

At first things went well. On the second day Ivan's warriors captured a band of Saxon scouts. One of the men was persuaded to talk. Alfred, he said, was at the royal palace of Westbury. He was planning to move along the edge of the Great Plain, then go north to surround

King Alfred

Chippenham. Guthrum immediately ordered his army to move south to cut him off.

That night the Danes camped near Edington, within sight of the plain. The following morning Guthrum called Ivan to him. 'Last time you went looking for Alfred, Ivan, you failed. Remember?'

Ivan looked annoyed. 'Of course, Guffrum. But that was different. He was hiding in a stinking bog, wasn't he?'

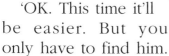

Ivan

'OK. This time it'll be easier. But you only have to find him. Then wait for me to join you. We'll attack together. Understand?'

'Yes. But if he's got only a tiny army, can I do the job myself?' Ivan asked eagerly.

Guthrum smiled. He liked Ivan, for all his bone-headedness. 'I'm afraid he hasn't got a tiny army, Ivan. So wait for me. I want to share in the fun.'

Ivan went back to his men. 'Right. Listen to me,' he barked. 'Guffrum says we have to find this Alfred. We can attack him if he has a tiny army. But if he has a lot of men, we must wait for the others. That's all, so let's get moving!'

Earl Athelnorth

Leaving their horses behind, Ivan's warriors spread out and began to climb the hill in front of them. After they had gone a few hundred paces, a band of Saxons rose up out of the grass ahead of them. They carried the banner of Earl Athelnorth.

The Danes shouted to Ivan for orders. He screwed up his eyes and looked carefully at the enemy. They were just a tiny army after all! 'Bad luck, Guffrum,' he chuckled. 'You were wrong!'

'Charge!' he yelled. 'Charge in the name of Odin! Cut the Saxon scum to pieces! But leave Alfred to me!'

Watching from below, Guthrum was helpless to stop the disaster. When the Danes were about twenty paces from the enemy, the banner of King Alfred suddenly appeared. Behind it thousands of Saxons moved out of the dip in which they had been hiding and hurled themselves at the astonished Danes.

After they had gone a few hundred paces,
a band of Saxons rose up out of the grass
ahead of them.

Ivan's men did not stand a chance. Many went down at the first charge. The rest were surrounded and hacked to pieces. Ivan fought with the strength of ten men until he too disappeared beneath the Saxon tide.

Guthrum could hardly bear to watch. 'O Great God Odin,' he muttered, 'what have I done to deserve this? It is the end of all my dreams.'

After seeing Ivan fall, he turned his horse and ordered his men to follow him back to Chippenham.

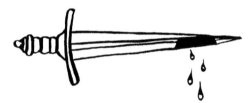

CHAPTER SEVEN

'WHY DID IT HAPPEN?'

Guthrum and his men made it safely back to the fort. A few of Ivan's warriors joined them during the night. Most, however, lay dead on the hillside at Edington.

The Saxon army appeared early the following morning. As Guthrum had feared, it was anything but a tiny army. There were thousands and thousands of them. Ploughmen from Wiltshire, Somerset sheep farmers, fishermen from the coastal villages of Hampshire. They were all well-armed and well-organised. As soon as they arrived, a tall man on a horse rode out and arranged them before the Danish fort.

Guthrum recognised the man immediately. He dressed like a king, sat his horse like a king, gave orders like a king. It could only be Alfred, King of Wessex.

After he had seen his enemy - so proud and so able - Guthrum lost interest in what was going on. Anund took over command of the fort. The king sat alone in his hut, eating almost nothing and refusing to talk to anyone.

For a couple of days even Ubbe stayed clear of Guthrum. Then, on the third morning, he went into the king's hut. 'Greetings, O Great Dane,' he called cheerily. 'What's it like being a shark?'

'Humph! Stop your stupid riddles, Fool!' said Guthrum grimly.

Ubbe the Fool

Ubbe sat on the table and tucked into the untouched royal breakfast. When he had polished off the last rasher of bacon, Guthrum finally asked, 'All right then, what do you mean?'

'Ah! Talking are we? Good. What I mean is this: we are the shark in the sea; the Saxons are the men on the land. Both are safe, as long as they stay where they are. If they come to get us, we'll eat them alive. If we go out to get them, they'll kill us. Stalemate.'

'What?'

'Stalemate. Oh, sorry. I forgot you don't play chess.'

Guthrum got up slowly. His face was lined with worry. 'Stop playing games with me, Ubbe. Tell me, why did it happen? Why did Odin let us down?'

Ubbe hesitated.

'Go on,' Guthrum repeated, 'tell me why Odin let us down.'

'Well,' said Ubbe carefully, 'have you ever thought that perhaps - only perhaps - there might not be an Odin after all?'

When Ubbe had polished off the
last rasher of bacon, Guthrum finally asked,
'All right then, what do you mean?'

Guthrum looked Ubbe straight in the eyes. 'That's what you think, isn't it?'

'Since you ask, yes. Odin would be a great idea if life were all fighting and so on. But I reckon there's a bit more to things than just blood and guts. I thought you were beginning to think that way, too. Before the battle. When you said you felt you had had enough of fighting.'

Guthrum thought for a moment before asking, 'Your song about not being able to kill Alfred's god - does it mean that you approve of this Christ person, this god of love the Saxons worship?'

Ubbe shrugged. 'Don't know much about him. But don't you think life *would* be better if we had a bit more love and mercy about the place? Better for cripples like me. Perhaps even for - er - old soldiers like you.'

Guthrum smiled. 'Maybe. So what do we do? Love can't get us out of the mess we're in.'

'But talking can, O King-Who-Is-Getting-Wiser-By-The-Minute. Alfred can't get you, and you can't get him. So what about a chat? You might be able to sort something out between you.'

'Would it be wise, Fool?'

'It would be the wisest thing you've ever done.'

'Very well. I'll try. I've always wanted to meet this Alfred.'

Ubbe the Fool

King Guthrum

CHAPTER EIGHT

TALKS AND SURPRISES

Ubbe made the first move. Calling over the river, he asked to speak with Earl Athelnorth. The Saxons thought it was a trick and did not reply. Ubbe tried again. This time one of the men ran off to find the earl.

For half an hour Ubbe and Athelnorth shouted at each other across the water. When

Earl Athelnorth

they had finished, Athelnorth said he would pass on the Danes' message to King Alfred.

The following day a large group of Saxons gathered by the river and called for Ubbe. He came, this time with Guthrum beside him. As neither side trusted the other, they agreed to hand over prisoners. If one side tried to trick the other, the prisoners would be killed. Two dozen Danes, including Anund, went into the Saxon camp. The same number of Saxons came into the fort.

The talks could now begin.

The Saxons put up a tent about one hundred paces from the fort wall. The rest of their army stood a long way off. A trumpet sounded. King Alfred came forward with two other men and entered the tent. When a second trumpet sounded, Guthrum and Ubbe walked out to meet the Saxon king.

Guthrum lifted the flap of the tent and went inside. Ubbe followed. Alfred was sitting behind a table. Behind him stood Earl Athelnorth and a priest named Plegmund. Alfred stood up and put out his hand. 'Welcome, King of the Danes,' he said warmly. 'May God be with you.'

Guthrum was amazed at the greeting. He had been expecting frowns and curses. Instead, he was being received with smiles and handshakes. He did not understand this sort of behaviour at all.

Earl Athelnorth   **King Alfred**   **Plegmund**

The two kings sat opposite each other and began talking. They spoke in Anglo-Saxon. The

Guthrum lifted the flap of the tent
and went inside.

Danish and Anglo-Saxon languages were quite similar. When Guthrum did not understand something, Ubbe helped him out.

The more they talked, the more Guthrum was surprised by Alfred. He was gentle yet firm. Some of Guthrum's suggestions he agreed to at once. Others he refused to accept. He seemed so clever, too. He knew all about the Danes and their adventures. He remembered dates and events. And as they talked, he made notes on a piece of parchment. Guthrum had never met a king who could read and write before.

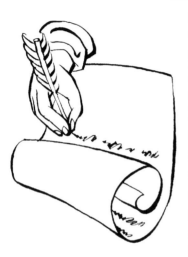

Alfred said it would be difficult to drive the Danes out of their fort. But, he pointed out, they could not leave unless he agreed.

He suggested an answer: he would let the Danes go, if they left Wessex and never returned.

Guthrum turned to Ubbe. 'What do you think, Fool?'

Ubbe nodded. 'You will not get a better offer, Sire.'

Ubbe the Fool

'Very well,' Guthrum said, 'I will leave Wessex to you, Alfred.'

'Thank you. It will be best for both of us.' Alfred paused. 'There is one other matter to discuss, Guthrum.'

'Yes?'

Alfred leaned back in his chair. 'I would like you to become a Christian.'

Plegmund and Earl Athelnorth watched Guthrum carefully. Ubbe shuffled his feet. Alfred sat completely still.

Plegmund   **Earl Athelnorth**

'I thought you were going to ask that,' Guthrum said slowly.

'And?' asked Alfred.

'I don't know much about your religion.'

'I can help you,' interrupted Plegmund. 'I shall give you the good news.'

Guthrum looked first at the priest, then at Alfred. A broad smile spread over his face. 'Alright. Tell me the good news. I'll become a Christian.'

Alfred rose to his feet. 'Let me embrace you, Guthrum! You are a great man!'

Maybe, said Ubbe to himself. But you, Alfred, are the greatest of them all.

King Alfred

WHAT HAPPENED NEXT?

PEACE

After the two kings had agreed to make peace, Alfred invited Guthrum to come and stay at Athelney. Guthrum accepted and they spent twelve days feasting and rejoicing.

The peace was set out at Wedmore, near Athelney. Guthrum and 30 of his men were baptised in the River Aller. The Danes finally left Wessex in October and went to Cirencester. Guthrum kept his word and did not attack Wessex again. He became king of East Anglia and died in 890.

THE REIGN OF KING ALFRED

The Peace of Wedmore did not end Alfred's troubles. He was often attacked by other groups of Vikings, but he managed to drive them away. To make Wessex stronger, he fortified important towns. They were known as 'burghs'. He also built ships to stop the Vikings attacking from the sea. During his reign Wessex got bigger. In 886 he took over London from Mercia.

Alfred was also an excellent scholar. This was very unusual for a king. He worked with priests to improve education. They translated important religious books from Latin into Anglo-Saxon, so more people could read them. Because he was a scholar, soldier and organiser, Alfred is known as Alfred the Great.

VIKINGS AND ANGLO-SAXONS

The fighting between the Vikings and the English went on long after Alfred's death. At first the English were very successful. Alfred's sons and grandsons conquered the Danelaw and became kings of all England. The Vikings then attacked again and in 1016 England had a Danish king, Cnut. The last big Viking attack on England was in 1066. The Vikings were not driven from Scotland until 1216.

Place names tell us where the Vikings settled in England. The Viking word *by*, for example, means a farm or village. So Denby is the 'farm of the Danes'. *Thorpe* also means farm or village. It gives us the name Grassthorpe, or 'grassy village'. Lots of ordinary Viking words came into the English language, such as *they*, *them*, *leg*, *egg* and *die*.

HOW DO WE KNOW?

In Anglo-Saxon times priests were almost the only people who could read and write. There were no newspapers and, of course, no TV or radio. So most of what we know about Alfred is what the priests said about him.

The most famous history is the *Anglo-Saxon Chronicle*. It was written by different priests in different monasteries over hundreds of years. The writers set down, year by year, what they thought were the most important events. They said a lot of kind things about King Alfred, because he was their hero! We now know that some of what they wrote was untrue.

Asser, a Welsh bishop who lived at Alfred's court, wrote a full story of Alfred's life. He made out the king to be a very holy, gentle man. In fact, he was a very tough soldier. Many of the details in Asser's book are incredible. He said, for example, that Alfred was handicapped. Some scholars think Asser's *Life* was not written by Asser at all. They say it was made up after Alfred died.

As the years went by, still more tales were made up about Alfred. They made him out to be even more of a hero. The most famous story (which is not true!) tells how he let a woman's cakes burn while he was hiding from the Danes at Athelney.

There are plenty of modern books written specially for children about Alfred and Anglo-Saxon times. Many have exciting pictures. See what you can find in your school or town library. You may also get a chance to visit some of the places where Alfred went. At Winchester there is a huge statue of him. It makes him look really great!

NEW WORDS

Banner Flag.
Club foot A foot that is the wrong shape.
Cotswolds Hills to the west of Oxford.
Deserted Empty.
Earl A nobleman.
Fosse Way A Roman road.
Gospel The Bible.
Heathen The Christian word for someone of another religion.
Latin The language of the Romans.
Monastry A place where monks live.
Odin The Viking's chief god.
Parchment Paper made of animal skin.
Pillage To take lots of things by force.
Plain A level piece of ground.
Plunder Something stolen in war.
Sod Earth.
Stalemate When a king can't move in chess.
Surround To cut a place off.
Vale A low valley.
Venison Deer meat.
Warband A group of soldiers.

Time line

About 400 Romans leave Britain. Tribes of Angles and Saxons begin to arrive.

597 St Augustine brings Christianity to Anglo-Saxon England.

793 The first Viking raid on England.

847 Alfred born.

853 Alfred goes to Rome, where he meets the pope.

865 Danish Great Army arrives in England.

866 Danes conquer Northumbria, Mercia and East Anglia.

871 Great Army attacks Wessex. Alfred and his brother King Ethelred defeat the Danes at Ashdown.
Ethelred dies. Alfred becomes king of Wessex.
Army of Wessex defeated. Alfred makes peace with the Danes.

877 Alfred makes peace after another Danish attack.

878 Guthrum takes Chippenham and conquers most of Wessex.
Alfred flees to Athelney.
Alfred defeats the Danes at Edington.
Guthrum makes peace with Alfred at Wedmore. He agrees to leave Wessex and become a Christian.

880 Guthrum king of East Anglia. England divided between Alfred's kingdom and the Danish lands, known as the Danelaw.

880s Alfred sets up fortified towns, known as burghs, across Wessex.

885 Alfred defeats Danes again.

886 London becomes part of Wessex.

890 Guthrum dies.

890s Danes attack Wessex again. Alfred defeats them easily.

893 Alfred re-organises his army.

897 Alfred's ships defeat the Danes.

899 Alfred dies and is buried in Winchester.

937 King Athelstan, grandson of Alfred, king of all England.

1116 Danish King Canute (or Cnut) ruler of all England.